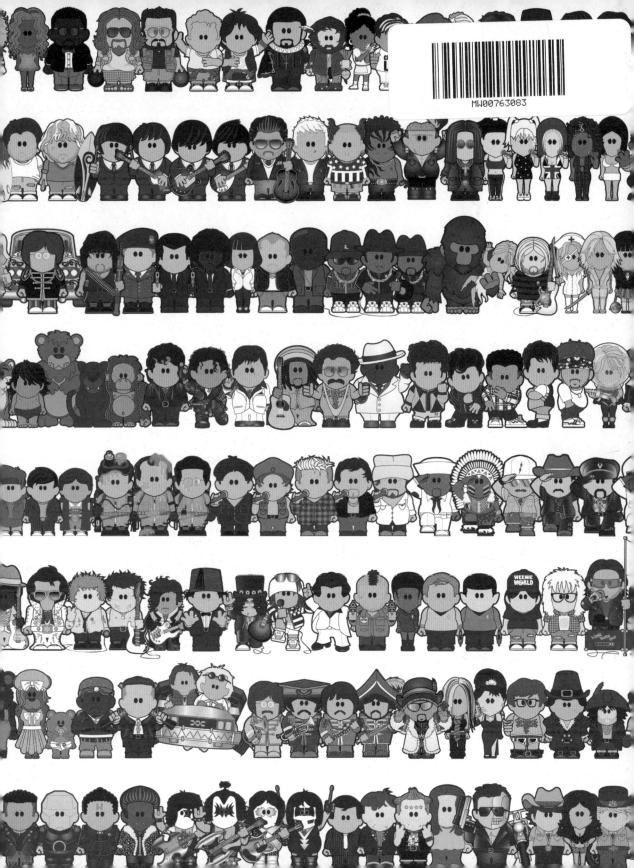

PRICE STERN SLOAN
Published by the Penguin Group
Penguin Group (USA) Inc, 375 Hudson Street, New York, New York 10014, USA
Penguin Group (Canada), 90 Eglinton Avenue East, Suite 700, Toronto, Ontario M4P 2Y3, Canada (a division of Pearson Penguin Canada Inc.)
Penguin Books Ltd, 80 Strand, London WC2R ORL, England
Penguin Group Ireland, 25 St. Stephen's Green, Dublin 2, Ireland (a division of Penguin Books Ltd.)
Penguin Group (Australia), 250 Camberwell Road, Camberwell, Victoria 3124, Australia (a division of Pearson Australia Group Pty Ltd.)
Penguin Books India Pvt. Ltd, 11 Community Centre, Panchsheel Park, New Delhi—110 017, India
Penguin Group (NZ), 67 Apollo Drive, Rosedale, Auckland 0632, New Zealand (a division of Pearson New Zealand Ltd.)
Penguin Books (South Africa) (Pty) Ltd, 24 Sturdee Avenue, Rosebank, Johannesburg 2196, South Africa

Penguin Books Ltd, Registered Offices: 80 Strand, London WC2R ORL, England

Published in the United Kingdom in 2011 as *Welcome to Weeniworld: An Intro to the Pop-Culture Planet!* by Penguin Books Ltd. First published in the United States in 2012 by Price Stern Sloan, a division of Penguin Young Readers Group, 345 Hudson Street, New York, New York 10014. PSS! is a registered trademark of Penguin Group (USA) Inc. Manufactured in China.

ISBN 978-0-8431-7093-1   10 9 8 7 6 5 4 3 2 1

ALWAYS LEARNING   PEARSON

WWW.WEENICONS.COM

Somewhere

in the depths of space,
hiding near the edge of the known galaxy,
exists a parallel universe. And in that universe, merrily orbiting
a smiley cartoon sun, is Weeniworld, the Pop Culture Planet.
It's like our planet earth, but smaller. And cuter. And cooler. And more fun.

WELCOME TO WEENiWORLD

PSS!
PRICE STERN SLOAN
An Imprint of Penguin Group (USA) Inc.

BOROUGH OF WEENIWORLD **WW10**

NOODLE BANGER ALLEY

BOROUGH OF WEENIWORLD **WW16**

VILE ISLE

BOROUGH OF WEENIWORLD **WW30**

FIVE CORNER SQUARE

HOLA, AMIGO! I BET YOU'RE WONDERING JUST WHAT YOU'VE STUMBLED
UPON? SI SI, WEENIWORLD CAN BE A CRAZY AND CONFUSING PLACE,
THAT'S FOR SURE. THERE'S A LOT ABOUT MY WEENI COMPADRES THAT
DOESN'T MAKE SENSE TO ME, AND A LOT ABOUT WHERE WE LIVE
THAT DOESN'T MAKE MUCH SENSE, EITHER. BUT MAYBE THIS IS WHAT
MAKES THE PLACE MORE LOCO THAN A TROUSERED ARMADILLO!
SO, VAMONOS! AND PREPARE FOR A BUMPY RIDE. I'LL GUIDE YOU
THROUGH MUCHOS CHAOS AS BEST I CAN.

¡VIVA LA WEENI REVOLUCIÓN!

Che

(FOUNDER OF WEENIWORLD)

BOROUGH OF WEENIWORLD **WW40**

BALMY BAY

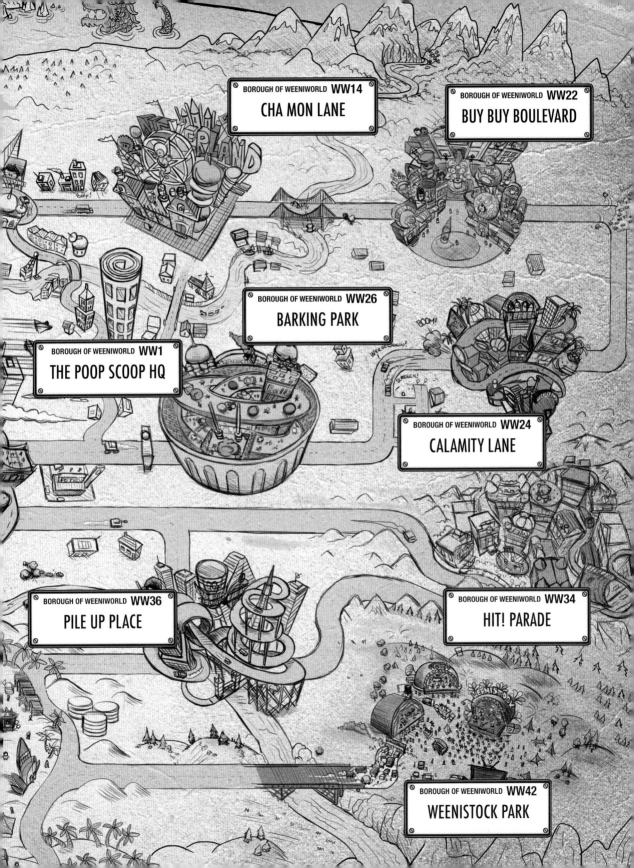

BOROUGH OF WEENIWORLD **WW14**
CHA MON LANE

BOROUGH OF WEENIWORLD **WW22**
BUY BUY BOULEVARD

BOROUGH OF WEENIWORLD **WW26**
BARKING PARK

BOROUGH OF WEENIWORLD **WW1**
THE POOP SCOOP HQ

BOROUGH OF WEENIWORLD **WW24**
CALAMITY LANE

BOROUGH OF WEENIWORLD **WW36**
PILE UP PLACE

BOROUGH OF WEENIWORLD **WW34**
HIT! PARADE

BOROUGH OF WEENIWORLD **WW42**
WEENISTOCK PARK

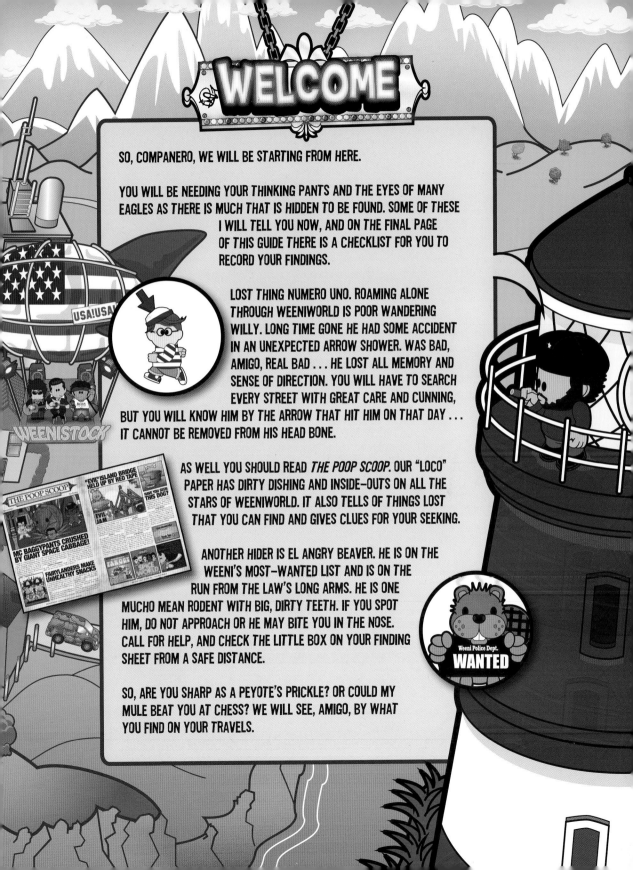

WELCOME

SO, COMPANERO, WE WILL BE STARTING FROM HERE.

YOU WILL BE NEEDING YOUR THINKING PANTS AND THE EYES OF MANY EAGLES AS THERE IS MUCH THAT IS HIDDEN TO BE FOUND. SOME OF THESE I WILL TELL YOU NOW, AND ON THE FINAL PAGE OF THIS GUIDE THERE IS A CHECKLIST FOR YOU TO RECORD YOUR FINDINGS.

LOST THING NUMERO UNO. ROAMING ALONE THROUGH WEENIWORLD IS POOR WANDERING WILLY. LONG TIME GONE HE HAD SOME ACCIDENT IN AN UNEXPECTED ARROW SHOWER. WAS BAD, AMIGO, REAL BAD . . . HE LOST ALL MEMORY AND SENSE OF DIRECTION. YOU WILL HAVE TO SEARCH EVERY STREET WITH GREAT CARE AND CUNNING, BUT YOU WILL KNOW HIM BY THE ARROW THAT HIT HIM ON THAT DAY . . . IT CANNOT BE REMOVED FROM HIS HEAD BONE.

AS WELL YOU SHOULD READ *THE POOP SCOOP*. OUR "LOCO" PAPER HAS DIRTY DISHING AND INSIDE-OUTS ON ALL THE STARS OF WEENIWORLD. IT ALSO TELLS OF THINGS LOST THAT YOU CAN FIND AND GIVES CLUES FOR YOUR SEEKING.

ANOTHER HIDER IS EL ANGRY BEAVER. HE IS ON THE WEENI'S MOST-WANTED LIST AND IS ON THE RUN FROM THE LAW'S LONG ARMS. HE IS ONE MUCHO MEAN RODENT WITH BIG, DIRTY TEETH. IF YOU SPOT HIM, DO NOT APPROACH OR HE MAY BITE YOU IN THE NOSE. CALL FOR HELP, AND CHECK THE LITTLE BOX ON YOUR FINDING SHEET FROM A SAFE DISTANCE.

SO, ARE YOU SHARP AS A PEYOTE'S PRICKLE? OR COULD MY MULE BEAT YOU AT CHESS? WE WILL SEE, AMIGO, BY WHAT YOU FIND ON YOUR TRAVELS.

OUR JOURNEY BEGINS WITH AN ORDINARY DAY IN AN EXTRAORDINARY PLACE. HERE ON NOODLE BANGER ALLEY, THE NOISY VOLUME IS ALWAYS TURNED UP TO ELEVEN! THE SUN IS SHINING AND THE WEATHER IS . . . WELL . . . MORE LOCO THAN A CACTUS TACO!

MC BAGGYPANTS CRUSHED BY GIANT SPACE CABBAGE!

"Arrghh! It's a Brassica Oleracea!" These were the last words MC Baggypants uttered (with a surprisingly impressive knowledge of botanical Latin!) before he was hit by a giant space cabbage. As ever, *The Poop Scoop* was on the scene to capture the very moment of leafy impact as the sky rained down gargantuan greenery.

This is not the first unusual weather occurrence over the last few weeks. Weeniworld has only just finished the clean-up from the intergalactic asparagus shower that landed on Balmy Bay last month.

CABBAGE-TASTROPHY!

We spoke to weather company "Purple Rain," who gave us the benefit of their meteorological expertise with this explanation: "We think that under precise and rare climatic circumstances, vegetable matter can condense in the air using pure green as a condensation nucleus. Or, simply put, some giant cabbages fell from the sky for some reason." As usual, we are now none the wiser.

FAIRYLANDERS MAKE UNHEALTHY SNACKS

Let's say you've invested in a magical storybook that harnesses the power of an entire fairytale kingdom to run your fantastic theme park. You'd want the Fairylanders to be in tip-top condition and full of energy, right?

Well, as everyone in Weeniworld knows, MJ has just such a book, and it's the power behind his Neverland funfair.

But now, in a never-before-revealed- totally-exclusive EXCLUSIVE we can reveal that the creatures exist solely on . . . COTTON CANDY!!!!! AND IT'S AFFECTING THEIR HEALTH!!!

"It's just so fluffy and yummy!" a fairytale representative murmured feebly, before keeling over.

So, if you notice your Neverland ride is going slow, join our campaign to Get Fairies Off Junk food NOW!! Before it's too late!

"EVIL" ISLAND BRIDGE HELD UP BY RED TAPE

HAVE YOU SEEN
THIS DOG?

Calling all eagle-eyed *Poop Scoop* readers! Weeni-Woman has once again misplaced Mr. Pickles, her invisible wonder pooch, and is possibly offering YOU a reward of mild gratitude if you happen to spot him.

STINKY BONE!

Last spotted outside Hammertime Hardware in Noodle Banger Alley, the tricky Mr. Pickles has a tendency to roam all over Weeniworld. Please inform us ASAP of any sightings. He might be in any street, at any time, doing anything with anyone! So our question is: can anyone SPOT an invisible dog? We wait with bated breath . . .

A temporary crisis was temporarily averted this week as the long-standing cracks in Boing Boing Bridge began to open up once again. Emergency measures had to be taken, so the Vile Islanders stuck the bridge back together with an enormous roll of red sticky tape and a spoonful of evil jam.

STICKY!!

Ever concerned about Weenicon safety, *The Poop Scoop* quizzed local evil genius, Doc Mong, about how long the tape would hold up.

"Well, the last time this happened we stuck it back together using bubblegum and lemon pudding and it held up pretty well for a couple of years," he answered, "so if I take the square root of jam and multiply the hypotenuse of sticky tape over gum, it should last anywhere between five minutes and a decade."

JAMMY!

Not everyone in Weeniworld was concerned by the idea of Dr. Meani and his Meanicon cronies struggling to make it over to the mainland, however. "I'd be happy to see the back of their poor excuse for jam," Dingo, from Pepperland Greengrocers, said in response to the crisis. "They must have some pretty sticky fruit on Vile Isle!" he added.

EVIL PRUNES!

Pondering this response leads to the obvious question: If you take Vile Isle cranberries and stew them like apple sauce, do they taste much more like evil prunes than rhubarb does? I put the question to head of Meanicons Corp., Dr. Meani, and he had this to say on the matter: "Eh? Go Away!"

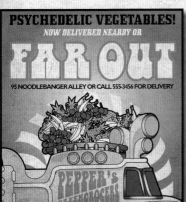
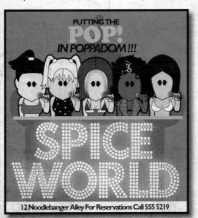

NOW, LET'S HEAD OVER TO NEVERLAND, SEÑOR MJ'S FANTASTICO FAIRYTALE THEME PARK! MJ HAS A SPECIAL STORYBOOK FULL OF MAGICAL FAIRYLANDERS WHO RUN THE PLACE. IT'S JUST A SHAME THEIR APPETITE FOR COTTON CANDY MAKES THEM MORE USELESS THAN A RATTLESNAKE'S SANDALS.

DR. MEANI'S DASTARDLY CREATION

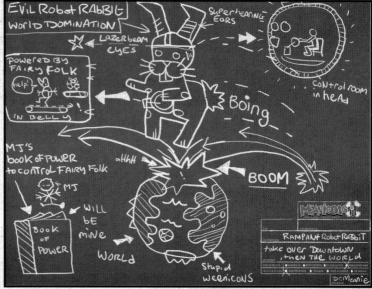

EXCLUSIVE

There is an ominous construction being built, which now looms large on the horizon of the Vile Isle.

BIG!!

We sent a terrified reporter to investigate and can now reveal, in another *Poop Scoop* exclusive, that Dr. Meani is planning something. Something bad. Which is not good.

PINK!!

Using our famous undercover techniques, we managed to get these exclusive pictures, showing what seems to be a plan for world domination using a big, dastardly pink mechanical rabbit. What is truly shocking, however, is that the plan appears to feature MJ and his book of magical Fairylanders!!

BUNNY!!

As these blueprints reveal, Dr. Meani once again has absolute power on his evil mind. It appears Dr. Meani plans to put the Fairylanders on treadmills to power his bunny-bot—and cause mayhem and general trouble in Weeniworld.

EVIL MJ??

Details on the blueprint seem to indicate MJ's involvement in the evil scheme. We

Blueprint Detail

spoke to our local expert who concluded that he is either a complete baddy, or totally innocent.

Either way, things are not looking good for Weeniworld. More on this breaking news as it happens . . .

GIRL POWER SAY "NO" TO WHOOPEE CUSHIONS

ANOTHER EXCLUSIVE

The GORGEOUS part-time singing troupe, Girl Power, are putting their weight (such as it is) behind a new campaign to ban the sale and promotion of whoopee cushions in Weeniworld!

DISGRACE!!

"It's such a disgrace that those awful things are pushed on children who don't know any better," said the posh one. "They cause so much upset and embarrassment, and what is funny about a . . . y'know, WINDY-TYPE NOISE anyway?" squeaked the little one.

To promote their cause, Girl Power are currently writing a song called "Let's Not Make Whoopee. . . . Just Say NO!!"

NO WHOOPEE!!!

"We're proud of the title cos it grabs your attention and it's sort of got a pun in it, innit," said the feisty one. "But," the girls chorused, "we don't want that to detract from the SERIOUS message. So we made sure it wasn't very funny."

The single, with all proceeds going to the J.S.N.T.W.C. society will, unfortunately, be available soon!

CAR-BAB!!

The Poop Scoop can reveal a SHOCKING new parking facility at Buy Buy Boulevard, Weeniworld's premier shopping center.

Anyone looking to park at Buy Buy will now have to leave their car on a SPIKY multi-story SKEWER!

I interviewed James, from "Hello Ladies Matchmaking Services," about the problem. "The fact that it leaves a hole in the roof and the floor of your car is a bit inconvenient," he answered, "but worse still, when my patented "Ladytron" has worked its magic and I want to leave early, if you know what I mean, then being at the bottom of a spike really doesn't help. Ladies don't like to wait!"

On the plus side, with the new initiative, parking charges are down to 300 Weeni Dollars an hour!

DOWNTOWN DINOS!!

Have YOU seen DINOSAURS in downtown Weeniworld lately?? Well, many Weenicons are making just such an outrageous claim! We have received literally three letters and the inconclusive photo above, all supporting a sighting of these pre-historic and long-extinct animals!

So far, The Poop Scoop's highly-trained reporters have not spotted any of these creatures, though we have been led to believe that they are a) masters of disguise and b) not in the habit of hanging out in Amy's Wine Bar.

So how have dinosaurs made it into Weeniworld? We went straight to the likely source, time traveler and crazy inventor, Doc, who claimed that it must be something to do with Space Cabbages as he absolutely, definitely had not left open any portals to any dimensions past or present, ever.

Our search for answers continues . . .

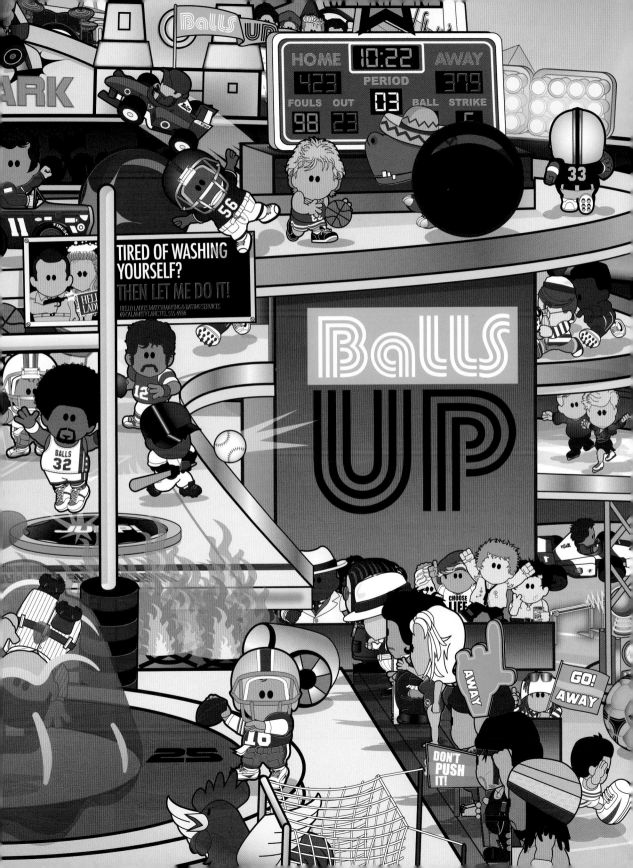

LOOK! MJ SHOOK BY BOOK CROOK!

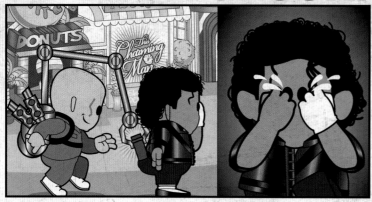

Weeniworld has been shaken by the sinister snatching of MJ's magical storybook! Our reporters were once again on hand to "scoop the poop" as these alarming pictures show. Now, the burning question for all Weenicons is: What dastardly plan has Dr. Meani got up his evil sleeve?

TEACUP!!

The theft of the book means not only that Dr. Meani has gained power over the Fairylanders but, more significantly, that this reporter will not be able to enjoy the thrills of the "Mad Teacup Ride" at Neverland this weekend.

MJ was understandably devastated. "Boo hooo, boo hoo," he said when questioned.

TABLE!!

So just what are Dr. Meani's intentions? We consulted an expert in evil genius psychology, who suggested the following: either he's planning devastating world domination and the destruction of all life as we know it OR he has an evil table with one short leg OR, just possibly, he's lost his Weeniworld library card.

CLUELESS!!

The Calamity Lane heroes have been put on full alert—so don't expect an early conclusion to this shocking story. More news as it comes in.

LACK OF BRAINS HINDERS RESEARCH

"Hmm . . . it's all about getting the oojamaflip parallel with the wotsit and then, erm, linked up with the COMBOBULATING BITS and, aaahh . . . mwha ha ha haaa . . . jelly . . ." mumbled Mong, the twin brother of Meani henchman, Ming.

COMBOBULATING!?

Or at least we think that's what he said. Weeniworld's Greatest Evil Scientist was expounding his plan to create life from bits and pieces found behind the Meanicon staff sofa. So far, the absence of a handy human brain has been causing problems, but a recent breakthrough involving electric currents and lime jelly could be the turning point, and nothing short of scientific revolution.

JELLY!!

But first, Mong has to work on the perfect consistency—too much wobble, and thoughts just aimlessly bounce around with no direction.

FUTURE!!

"I believe that I have seen the future, and the future is green evil jelly!" concluded the slightly baffling professor. The question remains: is this truly scientific progress? Or is this Meanicon scientist a few grapes short of a fruit salad?

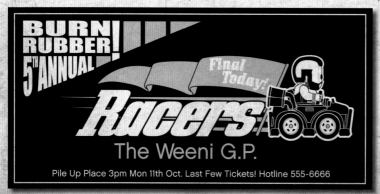

LOST VAN FOUND BY TREE!

Undercover renegade and part-time hermit, Jonny, is such a master of the art of camouflage that he has sometimes been known to lose himself. His most recent camo-tastrophe was misplacing an entire motorhome. "I'd been working on the paint job for hours, then looked away for a second and the van was gone!" he reported. After several days of searching, the ever-helpful Park Life garden team finally stumbled over Jonny's lost vehicle.

"When we heard that poor Jonny had lost ANOTHER van, well, we thought, oh no, this is a low!" they said. "As it turned out, the van looked like trees that like vans that like vans to be trees," which made the situation no clearer! Jonny and van have since been reunited . . . until the next time!

TEE AT BOILING POINT

Ardent anti-rug campaigner Tee is truly passionate about his cause. At a rally recently he shared his mission statement with our roving reporter:

"Have you ever tried to clean milk from a rug, fool? Those things get STINKY! They STAIN! They FRAY AROUND THE EDGES! We need to think of the children here, suckas! I will not rest, I will not sleep until Weeniworld is free of rugs. I see the future, and it has WIPE-CLEAN FLOORS!!!"

This morning his campaign reached a new level as an impassioned Tee cornered local rug merchant, Austin. Eager to convey the importance of his message, Tee wrestled the groovy gentleman and his mojo to the ground.

However, it is going to take more than random violence to get through to a lifelong rug user. Though his voice was muffled, our sharp-eared Weeni on the scene heard an unapologetic Austin questioning the very essence of Tee's mission:

"Why say no to rugs, man? They are SHAGADELIC, baby!!"

CITY GIRLS IN RAMPANT RABBIT SCARE

It was a narrow escape for our favorite shop "n" gossip posse today as they came within inches of being crushed by a bionic bunny beast.

BUNNY MAYHEM!

Downtown Weeniworld was in turmoil as Dr. Meani powered the mechanical monstrosity through the streets, destroying everything in his evil wake.

Our brave reporter was on hand, as ever, to capture the girls' reactions as they threw themselves out of the rampant rabbit's path. Unfortunately, their high-pitched screams caused his dictaphone to malfunction, but "EEEEEEEEEEEK!!" just about sums it up.

SPLAT!!

Moments after the girls dived for cover, the bunny froze in mid-hop before plunging to the ground in a twisted metal heap.

CREAM-CRACKERED!!!

We observed poor MJ's Fairylanders dragging themselves from the rabbit wreckage, clearly battered and exhausted by the experience. So, Dr. Meani's evil plans have once again come to nothing, although some serious damage has been reported by the City Girls, namely three broken fingernails and a scuffed heel.

HASTY WITHDRAWAL

The chase is now on to stop Dr. Meani from going into hiding in his lair on Vile Isle. He was last seen heading to Balmy Bay with his entourage of Meanicons.

Expect further updates on the chase for Meani as details emerge . . .

EVIL GENIUS NOT SO SMART

A recent shock revelation has shown that dastardly Dr. Meani may not actually be a bonafide evil mastermind after all.

We calculated today that he has now attempted a grand total of 3,896 evil plans and has a roughly-estimated success rate of 0.0356%.

BOO!!

Previous failures include the Slightly Grumpy Swampy Donkey, The Violent Toupee and the Ill-tempered Sea Bass with Laser Beam. All of which were rubbish.

After this latest failure, what next for Dr. Meani?

80s PHONE BOX SEEN ON THE MOON

After months of rumor and speculation about the rectangular object seen on the moon surface, it has been confirmed that it is indeed a phone box last used during the late 1980s.

All was revealed today as B&T Telecommunications confessed to the blunder, claiming that their experimental time-traveling phone booth took a "wrong turn at Saturn."

URANUS!

When asked why they were traveling through time and space, they claimed that they were on an important mission to discover if "there is indeed a ring of debris around Uranus, dude!" Most excellent!

DJ REVEALS BUST TO WEENIWORLD!

There was admiration and awe as DJ revealed her bust to an enthusiastic crowd of onlookers yesterday afternoon. It was unveiled to rapturous applause as part of the Balmy Bay Lifeguard of the Year award ceremony. One onlooker was heard to remark, "DJ's bust was so beautiful, it brings a tear to the eye."

FINISH

CRASH RATTLE & ROLL!

The Weeni GP finished moments ago and we are able to reveal the winner of this year's race.

SMASH!

Diamond Derek's Pina Colada Pineapple Bombs proved highly effective, as did Mikey's Giant Hood Smasher.

WELL-BRED!

Heroes for Hire's Evil-Seeking Shark-Faced Custard Missiles nearly won them the race, but once again they were thwarted by Tiffany's Absolutely Lovely Super-Polite Racer, which picked its way apologetically through a crowded track to stop in at the last moment and elegantly cross the line in first place.

The awards ceremony will take place at tonight's Weenistock festival.

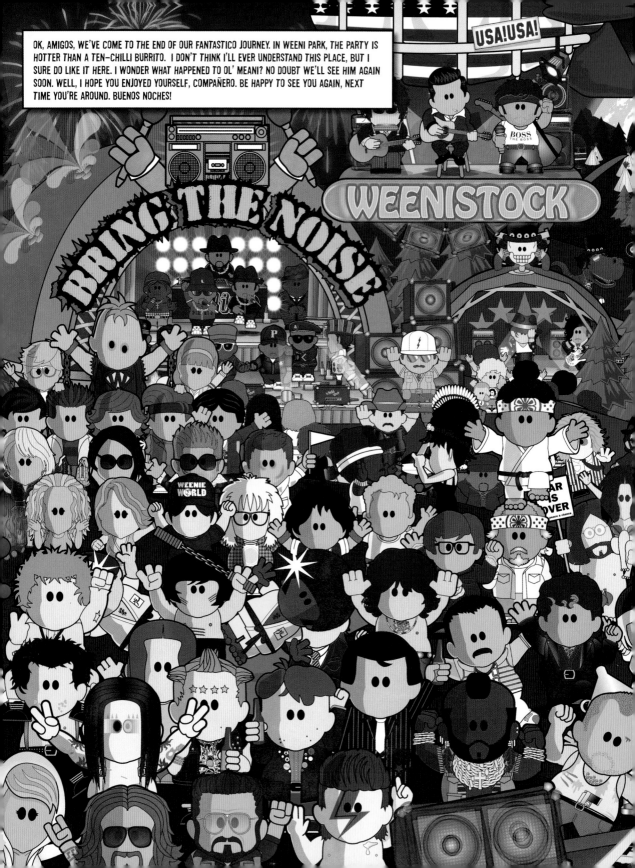

OK, AMIGOS, WE'VE COME TO THE END OF OUR FANTASTICO JOURNEY. IN WEENI PARK, THE PARTY IS HOTTER THAN A TEN-CHILLI BURRITO. I DON'T THINK I'LL EVER UNDERSTAND THIS PLACE, BUT I SURE DO LIKE IT HERE. I WONDER WHAT HAPPENED TO OL' MEANI? NO DOUBT WE'LL SEE HIM AGAIN SOON. WELL, I HOPE YOU ENJOYED YOURSELF, COMPAÑERO. BE HAPPY TO SEE YOU AGAIN, NEXT TIME YOU'RE AROUND. BUENOS NOCHES!